TEENAGE
MUTANT
NINJA
TURTLES® II:
THE SECRET OF
THE OOZE™

Other Teenage Mutant Ninja Turtles® books available in Yearling Books:

Teenage Mutant Ninja Turtles®
    (a novelization of the movie) by B. B. Hiller
Six-Guns and Shurikens by Dave Morris
Red Herrings by Dave Morris
Buried Treasure by Dave Morris
Dinosaur Farm by Dave Morris
Splinter to the Fore by Dave Morris

Yearling Books/Young Yearlings/Yearling Classics are designed especially to entertain and enlighten young people. Patricia Reilly Giff, consultant to this series, received the bachelor's degree from Marymount College. She holds the master's degree in history from St. John's University, and a Professional Diploma in Reading from Hofstra University. She was a teacher and reading consultant for many years, and is the author of numerous books for young readers.

For a complete listing of all Yearling titles, write to
Dell Readers Service
P.O. Box 1045
South Holland, IL 60473.

TEENAGE MUTANT NINJA TURTLES® II:
THE SECRET OF THE OOZE™

A Novelization by B. B. Hiller
Based on the screenplay by
Todd W. Langen

A YEARLING BOOK

Published by
Dell Publishing
a division of
Bantam Doubleday Dell Publishing Group, Inc.
666 Fifth Avenue
New York, New York 10103

The trademark Yearling® is registered in the U.S. Patent and Trademark
Office.

The trademark Dell® is registered in the U.S. Patent and Trademark Office.

ISBN: 0-440-40451-7

Printed in the United States of America

April 1991

10 9 8 7 6 5 4 3 2 1

CWO

For my sons, Emmons & Andrew

1

"Call me Keno," the young man told his boss, the owner of the pizzeria where he worked. He did a good job as a delivery man and didn't like being called "Yo!"

His boss nodded. "Sure, Keno," he said. "Now, saddle up. We've got another order for that O'Neil lady."

"Are you kidding me? Again? That lady ought to get it wholesale! Plus, she's a lousy tipper!"

"Get going," Ray said, handing him a stack of pizzas.

Keno slid the boxes into the warmer attached to the back of his moped and shifted the bike into gear. Although he delivered pizzas to April O'Neil all day long, he'd never really seen her, except on television. She was a reporter for Channel 3. He wondered how she could eat so much pizza and still be so thin.

Keno stopped in front of Miss O'Neil's apartment building, got off the bike, and picked up the pizza

warmer. It was late at night and the street was dark and empty. It was quiet, too. The silence seemed a little strange in the middle of such a big city.

Then the silence was interrupted by an odd thudding sound. If Keno was anything, he was curious. Miss O'Neil could wait just a minute for her three pizzas while he checked out the noise.

It seemed to be coming from the rear of an electronics store next to Miss O'Neil's apartment house. He followed the alleyway between the buildings. Keno walked silently, hiding in the shadows, though it was hard because he was still carrying the pizza. He stopped and peered around the corner of the building to see the source of the thudding.

It wasn't just thudding. What Keno saw was a couple of stocking-masked thugs carrying big boxes out of the electronics store. There was a robbery in progress!

Keno wasn't afraid. He knew what to do.

"All right, hold it!" he called out from the shadows. "You guys are under arrest!"

The thugs looked into the shadows.

"What are you? Private security?"

Keno had their attention. He emerged from the dark corner, still holding the pizza warmer.

"Well, no," he began somewhat sheepishly. "I'm actually pizza delivery."

The thugs took that as an invitation. They put down the televisions they were loading and attacked.

Keno put the pizzas on the ground and defended himself. He dispatched the first attacker with a roundhouse kick. The next required two punches and a flip. A third, attacking from behind, got a reverse kick to his stomach, followed by an arm sweep that delivered him to the middle of a heap of boxes.

"Did I mention that I study martial arts?" Keno asked the unconscious bodies that surrounded him.

He was answered by the arrival of the rest of the stocking-masked thugs. Seven men attacked him at once. There weren't enough martial arts in the city for one man to counter that—even one as good as Keno was.

He punched, thrusted, kicked, and leapt, but he was worried.

"Help?" he called out feebly, knowing there was no way anybody was going to help him out of this mess.

Suddenly, though, his attackers were distracted. There was something behind Keno—something that *was* going to help him.

Then everything went dark. Keno was shrouded by a big, smelly dropcloth.

"Hey!" Keno protested.

"Sorry, kid, it's for your own good!" said a strange voice. The next thing Keno knew, he was wrapped up and tied like a Christmas present. Then somebody, or something, pushed him into a nearby garbage can for safekeeping!

Keno didn't know what was going on, but he listened.

"Oomph!"

"Awesome!"

"Umph!"

"Wicked!"

Smack!

"Eclectic!"

"Eclectic?"

Thunk!

Listening didn't help. He still didn't know what was going on!

2

They were young. They were green. They were a little bit strange, but they were definitely an awesome foursome. They were the Teenage Mutant Ninja Turtles.

Michaelangelo peered through his orange mask at the thieves Keno had been fighting.

"Boy, I really hate it when guys wear panty hose," he complained to Donatello while swinging his nunchakus.

Donatello, wearing a purple mask, slammed against one of the thugs with his *bo*—a ninja staff.

"You know, you should try Sheer Energy," Donatello advised the thug, who crumpled at the blow. "It'll make your face feel less tired at the end of the day!"

Don and Mike winked at each other and finished off the thugs.

Nearby, Raphael took out three thieves by himself and whisked his *sai,* three-pronged daggers, at a fourth, who was waiting for his own defeat.

"Man, this is too easy," Raphael complained to Leonardo, who was working next to him.

Leonardo got an idea. "Hey! Splinter says the true ninja is a master of his environment. Stow your weapons!"

"I'm game!" Raphael agreed. He tucked his *sai* into his red sash. He loved his *sai,* but he could fight without them, too, and this would be more fun.

Leonardo, who always fought with *katana,* long ninja swords, slid them into their scabbards across his back. He attacked with punches and kicks. It was all he needed.

Michaelangelo found himself fighting off three thugs at once. They backed him right through a plate-glass window into a delicatessen. When he looked up, all he could see were sausages and salamis.

"Great," he said to himself. "These guys have knives, and I've got cold cuts!"

Then he got an idea. He plucked a string of frankfurters from a hook above him and began whirling them—just like his beloved nunchakus. That was being a master of his environment!

"Good thing it was hard salami," he told the motionless form of the final thug.

Donatello crashed through the door of a toy store. Five thugs were hot on his tail. He looked for something to master. All he saw was a yo-yo. It was enough. Slipping the loop over one of his three fingers, he disarmed the first attacker with a "shoot the moon," and two more by snapping the toy in the classic "round the world." The thieves never knew what hit them. The other two ran for their lives. Don looked at the box the yo-yo came in. "Hmmm—'Safe for indoor use,'" he read.

"Your serve," Leonardo said, picking up a tennis racquet. He was in a sporting goods store. He faced off with one of the stocking-masked thugs.

The thug swung wildly at Leo. He missed.

"Love-fifteen," Leo announced as if he were scoring a tennis match.

The racquet swung past him again.

"Love-thirty. Keep your elbow stiff," Leo advised.

The thug grunted with anger. Then he used every bit of his power and swung at Leo again.

Leo ducked. "No, no. Follow through more. Love-forty."

This time, the thug tried to bring the racquet straight down on Leo. Leo stepped aside. The racquet smashed to the floor and shattered.

"That's game," Leonardo told the infuriated thug. "Well, look, you gave it your best shot."

Leo offered him his hand, as if to shake it, just the way tennis players did at the end of a match. The confused thug instinctively responded and reached for Leo's hand. Leo grabbed the hand and yanked the thug toward him. He then smashed his own racquet down over the thug's head. The thug fell to the ground, unconscious.

Even Leo was surprised that old ploy had worked. "Rent a brain cell!" he told his inert opponent. Leo was then distracted by the familiar sounds of a basketball game taking place on the next aisle.

Raphael dribbled the ball, feinted to the right, moved to the left. His stocking-masked opponent was quick enough to get right in Raph's path. Raph tossed the ball aside and delivered a punch to the thug's midsection, doubling him over. Raph picked him up and, using a trampoline for extra bounce, tossed the bewildered thug up, over, and right into the basket, where he dangled.

"Yes!" Raph cried out. "There it is! Raphael wins it! The crowd goes wild, the world goes crazy. They name a sneaker after him! He demands a new contract!"

Leo slung a congratulatory arm across Raph's shoulders and the two of them made their way out of the sporting goods shop and back into the alley. They found Mike on a pogo stick, chasing down the few remaining thugs. They joined in.

Raph noticed that the dropcloth on the trash can was beginning to open up. The pizza delivery boy was about to emerge—and that could mean trouble for him.

The last flap of fabric was pushed away and the first thug came up to attack.

"Hey, kid, look out! You're going to get—"

Raph didn't have time to finish. Keno sprang up from his crouch and delivered a deadly kick to the thug's jaw.

Keno turned to Raph. "You were saying?"

Being smug didn't help Keno at all. While he was

gloating, two more thugs attacked. Leo helped Keno. He delivered them to the pile of defeated thieves.

"He was saying you're going to get hurt. Now, get out of here and let us take care of this!"

Keno hesitated.

"Look, kid, go find a phone," Raph advised him. "Some of these guys are going to be waking up soon. Call the police. We'll start tying them up."

"But—" Keno protested. It didn't work.

"Yeah, yeah, but go!"

It took Keno only a few minutes to make the call. Then he ran back to the alley, refreshed and ready to start fighting again.

But there was no fighting to be done. All he found there were dozens of thieves, tied up and hanging, like ornaments, from the lampposts.

He did find something else. He found his pizza warmer was empty. All it had in it was money to pay for the missing pizza, plus a lousy tip!

3 ═══════════════════════

April unlocked the door of her apartment and peered in. It was a disaster area. Sharing a home with Teenage Mutant Ninja Turtles—even on a temporary basis—meant that you always had company, you always had pizza, and you always had a mess.

She picked up a monkey wrench, two hex nuts, and an awl. She put them in a toolbox, shut it, and stowed it in a closet. "Donatello," she said.

She moved a chair that had been jostled out of place by an athletic leap. "Leonardo," she noted.

She collected the comic books that were all over the floor and stacked them in a pile. "Raphael," she remarked.

She folded up an empty pizza box and put it in the trash. "Michaelangelo," she said, identifying the fourth houseguest. She sighed. The place was still a mess. "The *rat's* the clean one!"

The door flew open and the culprits bounded in.

"Primo workout, dudes!" Michaelangelo declared. He flopped into the chair April had just straightened.

"Muy primo, bros," Leo confirmed.

"Maxamundo!" Raphael added. He tossed all the sofa pillows on the floor and stretched out on them.

April watched the mess reappear before her eyes.

"Hey, guys," she began, hesitantly. She loved the Turtles and didn't like to criticize them, but her home was becoming an invasion site.

"Yo, April, what-it-is?" Raphael asked amiably.

"We brought dinner," Donatello said, before April could begin to explain.

It was pizza. Again.

Michaelangelo opened the box and inhaled the sweet smell of his favorite food.

"Time's up. Let's eat," Michaelangelo announced.

Raph took a bite, swallowed, and then began reliving the exciting battle they'd just had in the alley with the thugs and Keno.

"Hey, did you see the way I took down that one dude back there?"

Leonardo was not impressed, or at least he didn't want Raphael to think he was impressed. "Yeah, big deal. That move's easy to counter."

"You want to try?" Raphael challenged.

Before April knew what was happening, Raph and Leo were standing on the sofa, reenacting a ninja battle—with pizza for weapons.

"Guys. *Guys!*" she said, interrupting the fray. "I've got a lot of reading to do for an interview tomorrow, so I'd appreciate it if you could maybe stop?"

It didn't work. The battle continued.

"So," she said, trying another tack. "Any luck finding a new place to live yet?"

That worked.

"Not really," Don said. "It's hard to find good subterranean housing."

April could understand that. The Turtles were staying with her because their own home, in the sewers of the city of New York, had been discovered and overrun in a battle. The Turtles had been attacked by The Foot Clan. That was an evil ninja band run by Shredder, an old enemy of their own ninja master, a mutant rat named Splinter.

"We could always go back to the sewer den," Raph said, trying to be helpful and realizing that they were imposing on April, just a little.

"Yeah, right, Raph," Leo said. "It's a little tough when about five hundred members of The Foot Clan know where you live."

"We beat them but good that last time," Raph reminded his brother. "They're all in jail. And besides, we definitely took out the Shredder. What's everybody so worried about?"

"Correction there," Leo said. "*Splinter* took out the Shredder."

"Yeah, yeah. Get technical on me, Leo," Raph said.

"Well, he's the one who put Shredder over the rooftop," Leo reminded him.

Raph walked over to April's window and looked out, remembering Shredder's final battle. It seemed he could still see Shredder, wearing his shining razor-sharp armor, tumble four stories down, into the back of a garbage truck.

Raph stood up on the ledge as if he were about to reenact Shredder's tumble. "He did a swan dive with a half gainer . . ."

"Raphael! Come away from the window!"

Raph hopped down from the windowsill obediently and turned to face the voice of his master. Splinter, an aged four-foot-tall rat, stood at the railing of the loft of April's apartment. It overlooked her living room.

"Never forget who you are." Splinter spoke sternly to Raphael and his brothers. "You are ninja. You must *always* practice the art of invisibility. All of you."

"I don't get it," Raph said. "I mean, why? We saved the city. Why can't we just, you know, have some fun? Get some glory."

Splinter sighed. He'd been through this before. He suspected he would go through it again.

"Stand before me, my sons." The Turtles gathered and waited. "For fifteen years you have been confined below. Now the outside world beckons your teenage minds."

What he said was true and all of the Turtles knew it.

"But the people out there could never understand you. Their world is ours to protect, but it can never be ours to live in."

Michaelangelo paled. "Not even pizza?" he asked.

"Pizza's okay," Splinter said, smiling at the Turtles he'd come to think of as his family, his sons.

"Man, give a guy a heart attack!" Michaelangelo said with relief.

"Hey, Mikie, toss me another slice," Raph said now that the serious mood was broken.

Mike did just that. A gooey tomato, cheese, mushroom, pepper, and sauce-laden slice flew through the air toward Raph and toward April's brand-new white sofa.

"Uh, Mike, be care—"

Raph whipped out his *sai* and speared the flying pizza slice one millimeter before it landed on the sofa.

"—ful," April finished.

"Take heart, child," Splinter said. "We will not be here much longer."

April was embarrassed. She didn't want her guests to think she didn't want them there. On the other hand . . .

"Oh, no, you guys can stay." She gulped. "As long as you want."

"Hey, cool, I kind of like it here."

"No," Splinter said somberly. "We do not belong above."

"Yes, Master Splinter," Leonardo said obediently.

Raphael mimicked him. Splinter saw it happen.

"Hut! Ten flips. Now!" he commanded.

Obediently, Leo and Raph began doing flips.

"One . . . two . . . three. . ." they counted together.

Splinter walked toward the window, listening to his students count. "Such energy is wasted," he said, speaking to himself as well as to the Turtles. "Remember, the true ninja is a master of all things. A master of his environment. A master of *himself.* Focus your thoughts on where we must go and leave the Shredder buried."

4

The last garbage truck dumped its final load of the day and pulled away from the landfill. The towers of garbage seemed to mock the towers of the nearby city, which had created this vast wasteland of refuse.

Here and there rats scurried through the refuse, in search of another tidbit. Nobody saw them. As darkness fell, the crickets chirped hopefully. Nobody heard them.

A mound of garbage shifted. Orange rinds and disposable diapers tumbled, at first slowly, then faster, helter-skelter. A rat paused, curious. The glint of a piece of shiny metal caught its eye. The metal moved. It sparkled in the sparse starlight. Frightened, the rat fled.

The metal moved again. It emerged from the heap of garbage. It was a ninja spike, attached to a glove covering a hand. The full hand, and then an arm, came up out of the heap of rubbish. Methodically, the arm and hand began to brush away trash, eventually uncovering a whole person. He struggled against the forces of exhaustion and pulled himself clear of the heap that had nearly taken his life.

He was a large man. He was tall and strong. He was completely clothed in ninja armor, covered from head to toe with deadly spikes that were razor-sharp.

His name was Shredder and he was very much alive.

5

On the other side of the city there was a junkyard. It was filled with discarded metallic scrap. A small ramshackle cabin stood near the entrance. Inside the cabin there were a few young men, still dressed in their tattered black *dogi*—ninja outfits. They were all that was left of The Foot.

"Is this it?" one of them asked another.

His friend shrugged. "Everybody else must have been picked up by the police," he said.

"Maybe the others just couldn't find us," the first said, hoping that more of the clan had survived their battle with the Teenage Mutant Ninja Turtles.

"We *all* knew this junkyard was our fallback spot."

"*Nngghhhh!*" said Tatsu, Shredder's enforcer. It was his way of calling the ragtag group to attention. He wasn't much of a talker, but he managed to get his message across.

"Our father . . . gone! *Nggh!*" He smashed a

sawhorse with his fist. "They will pay! *Aiee!*" He splintered a wooden table with the side of his hand. "I, Tatsu, now lead. Let any who challenge step forward."

Tatsu once again raised his fist to smash something—this time a chair. He brought the fist down with all his force, but it was stopped, in midair, by another.

"*I* challenge," the intruder said solemnly.

The Foot Clan looked up.

"His face," said one.

"His voice," said another.

"Master Shredder," said Tatsu. He fell to his knees. They all bowed in obedience.

It didn't take long for Shredder to share his plan with The Foot Clan.

"Select the best man from those that remain," he told Tatsu. "I want him to follow the reporter. She is the key to finding the creatures that did this to me." He pointed to his soiled suit and his crumpled armor.

"And next, Master? We rebuild The Foot?"

"No. There is only one thing next." He narrowed his eyes and spoke slowly, savoring the word. "Revenge!"

6

April faced the television camera and smiled. She was standing in the middle of a chemical waste dump. It wasn't easy to smile there, but she had an interview to do and she had the feeling it was an important interview.

". . . and in this day and age of ecological abuse, it's nice to find a company that's doing something to help," she told the camera. Then she turned to the man next to her. He was a professor, and was wearing a workman's coverall with the initials T.G.R.I. on the pocket.

"Joining me on the final day of their cleanup efforts is Techno-Global Research Industries spokesman Professor Jordan Perry. Good afternoon, Professor."

Professor Perry smiled nervously. "Good afternoon, Miss O'Neil."

"Professor, perhaps you can tell us why T.G.R.I. has finally decided to remove the waste it's been burying here for years."

Professor Perry took a deep breath. "Well," he began. "I should try to keep my answers short, or will you be able to cut this later on, just in case I begin to ramble, which, unfortunately . . ."

"Uh, Professor. We're live," April said, reminding him that their talk was being broadcast right then.

"Oh, right," he said sheepishly. "Well, to answer your excellent question . . ."

"Man, who is this spasmatic?" Raphael said, talking to the television he and his brothers were watching in April's apartment. He felt sorry for April. He felt sorrier for himself, having to watch the whole thing.

"Hey, give the guy a break," Don said. "He's a scientist."

". . . Our organization has always been concerned with the welfare of the community we serve," the professor babbled.

"Isn't Oprah on?" Raphael asked.

"Just leave it," Don said. "We're watching April."

". . . and, yes, we have been depositing certain waste material—nontoxic, of course—at this particular site, but we now have more efficient ways of dealing with this waste . . ."

"How about Supermarket Sweep?" Raph suggested. "I hear they're having a special on garden hoses?"

". . . and so, at our own expense, T.G.R.I. has elected to remove these by-products and dispose of them in a more suitable way. . . ."

Raphael had just about had it. "Come on. Let's change this. Maybe somebody's got something on the fight at the electronics store last night." He reached for the remote.

"Do not change the channel," Splinter commanded from behind the Turtles. Raphael hadn't even known he was there. They all turned to look at him. He seemed very upset by something he'd seen.

The professor smiled at April again. "And that's really about all there is to it, Miss O'Neil," he said.

April smiled back, but she didn't believe him. "Thank you," she said politely. Then she faced the camera again. "Reporting live from New Jersey, this is April O'Neil, Channel Three Eyewitness News."

As soon as the camera light went off, April handed her microphone to one of the crewmembers and walked quickly to catch up with the professor. There was something that just didn't seem right.

"Would you mind if I asked a few follow-up questions?"

"Not at all," the professor said agreeably. Then he glanced at his watch. "Darn," he said. "Perhaps another time, Miss O'Neil." Almost before she knew what had happened, he'd gone. Now she was surer than ever that there was something he didn't want her to know. Disappointed, she returned to the sound truck, where her newest production assistant, Freddy, was coiling up some cables.

"Enjoying your first day, Freddy?" she asked.

"Sure," he said. "But tell me. What were you going to ask him?"

"Well . . ." April began, wondering if she could even explain. "I don't know," she said finally. "Don't worry about it, though. I'm paid to be suspicious."

7 ═══════════

Freddy was being paid to be suspicious, too, but not just by Channel Three News. On a hunch, he followed Professor Perry, and when he saw him talking to two men and sending them off toward a wooded area, Freddy followed them.

He crouched and ran through the grass silently. When the men stopped in a little glade at the edge of the waste site, Freddy ducked behind a rock.

"How could you have missed this?" one of the T.G.R.I. workers said to the other.

"I don't know." The other shrugged.

The first man took a measuring tape and began spouting figures. The other man jotted them down on a clipboard.

"Grab some men. I'll go find the professor. We've got to take care of this *now.*" He sounded urgent.

The two men left.

When they had gone, Freddy crept over to the little glade where they had been. It didn't take any time at all for him to see what had upset them, for there, in front of him, was a dandelion patch. They weren't just dandelions, though. They were each about the size of a volleyball. They were mutant dandelions!

Freddy plucked one very carefully and carried it back to the truck. He didn't want anybody—especially a suspicious news reporter—to see it.

Professor Perry shook his head in dismay when his assistant showed him the mutant dandelion patch.

"Hmmm. If the soil's been contaminated this far away, there must be more leaky canisters than we thought."

"But how can that be?" his assistant asked. "They were only buried fifteen years ago."

"Fifteen. Fifty. It doesn't matter. Just make sure the evidence is removed," he said.

"Maybe it wasn't such a good idea to invite the press."

"I don't agree," Professor Perry said. "Sometimes the best way to hide something is right out in public."

"But if any of it fell into the wrong hands . . ." the assistant said ominously.

"I'm aware of the risks," the professor said sharply.

In a junkyard, on the other side of the river, the wrong hands held a mutant dandelion. Those hands were covered with black gloves, spiked with ninja armor.

Shredder turned the dandelion around and examined it carefully.

"This isn't the reason I sent you to follow her," Shredder said to Freddy.

The tone of his master's voice made Freddy nervous. "No, Master," he said, desperately afraid of Shredder's anger. "But I . . ."

"Silence!" Shredder commanded.

Freddy was afraid Shredder could hear his heart beating.

"This may be even better. . . ." Shredder said.

Freddy's heart slowed down.

"Whatever caused this *mutation* may be useful against my enemies. Tatsu!"

Tatsu snapped to attention. "*Ngggh,*" he said agreeably.

"Gather your best men. You have a mission tonight."

"*Ngggh!*"

8

April's apartment was still a mess, but it was getting to be less of a mess than it had been. The Turtles were using all their ninja skills to clean it up.

Donatello cleaned with a mop as well as he fought with his *bo.* Leonardo had a dust rag on the tips of his *katana* swords. He could even dust the chandelier that way. Raphael speared litter with his *sai.*

"Hey, guys, check this out!" Michaelangelo said. He had a can of furniture polish in one hand, a rag in the other. He sprayed April's table and began buffing. "Wax on. Wax off."

Raphael tossed a soggy sponge at him.

"Mouth off," he said. It worked.

The door opened and April walked in. She couldn't help but notice the Turtles' efforts—including a five-foot-high stack of empty pizza boxes.

"Thanks, guys," she said, smiling. "Say, where's Splinter?"

"He's been up on the roof of the building ever since he saw your report. I don't know what he's doing up there—"

"Coming to a decision." Splinter spoke from the windowsill, where he was standing.

Leonardo bowed to him. "You've been meditating many hours, Master Splinter."

"Yes. And it is time. Join me above," Splinter said.

Without question, the Turtles followed him up the fire escape. April came, too.

"These last hours have been spent pondering many questions," Splinter began. "Some are the very questions of our origin: the sewer. Our transformation."

Raphael was curious about what Splinter was going to say, but he couldn't help thinking that Splinter could be almost as tedious as April's Professor Jordan Perry. He kept this thought to himself.

"But the answers have always remained hidden in the past, veiled by a shadow too deep to penetrate. Until now."

Raphael and his brothers were curious.

"A light from the present reaches back to illuminate that shadow." Splinter reached into his cloak and removed an old canister, broken into two pieces.

"You have never seen this, but know what it is."

"That's the canister that had the ooze—" Leonardo began excitedly.

"That transformed us all," Splinter finished for him. "I have kept it all these fifteen years."

"But why do you show it to us only now, Master Splinter?" Leonardo asked.

Splinter held the two pieces, one in each hand, Slowly he rotated them, fitting them back together as a whole. That was when the Turtles and April could read the label that had been split when the canister cracked.

"T.G.R.I.!" April said excitedly. "I knew it! I *knew* there was something else going on with those guys!"

"Yes," Splinter agreed. "And we must know exactly what it is. For if the contents of this canister are not unique, the city may now face grave danger."

The significance began to sink in. The Turtles had always enjoyed the things that made them different from the rest of the world. Even though they were clearly mutants and different from everybody else, they'd been able to use their differences for good purposes. They had no trouble living with their present. It was their past that was hard for them. They were always eager for some kind of hint or explanation about their origin.

Donatello thought of these things as he looked at the canister in Splinter's hand. "Not knowing who we are—*how* we are—"

"The past returns, my sons," Splinter said. "It is time to seek our answers."

9

Professor Perry sat alone at his work station. The glimmer of his computer screen cast an eerie light on a canister. It was identical to the one Splinter had shown the Turtles. The only difference was that this one wasn't broken. It was filled with a glowing green ooze.

"Well, you're the last one, aren't you?" the professor asked the canister. It shimmered in response.

The professor checked the serial number on the canister against his computer screen. It definitely was the last one.

"I'm afraid your trouble-making days are over," he said. He was ready to destroy it, to turn the bubbling radioactive goo into a harmless substance. The chemical apparatus to do the job was waiting.

He reached for the canister. It wasn't there.

"What the—?"

It was the last thing he said before a pair of black-gloved hands grabbed him and muffled his scream.

10

The Turtles landed almost silently on the rooftop of the T.G.R.I. laboratory.

Donatello looked around, checking out the unimpressive setup. He was disappointed to think that the answer to the question about his origins could lie in such a humble building.

"Not much to this place," he said.

Leonardo's thoughts were completely on the task, not its meaning. "Keep on your toes. It doesn't look like there's any night security, but we'd better move in quietly—"

"Duhhhh," Raphael said. He was impatient for the hunt. He didn't have time for Don's emotional approach or Leo's leadership. This was a time for action. "Come on, let's do it," he urged his brothers.

Michaelangelo found the open window. In a matter of seconds, all four of the Turtles were in.

Don was relieved to see the impressively large

room. This was more like it. "So, what do you guys think we'll find? You know, about us? Whatever it is, I bet it'll be special."

Mike looked around. The room was big, but it didn't seem to have any answers. "Yeah, either that, or we got the wrong address." His eyes caught the glow of a computer screen. Then he saw a lot of impressive chemical equipment. *"Hello!"* he said. The foursome crept silently to the corner of the lab where, just a few minutes before, Professor Perry had been finishing his work.

Don's eyes lit up as they approached the area. He loved mechanical, scientific things. His brothers looked at him for an explanation.

"I've no idea what all this is for," he said.

"Mondo video games?" Mike suggested, pointing to a joystick.

Don made a face. This was no time for jokes.

"Hey, some of this stuff seems to be running," Leonardo said.

"Yeah," Raph confirmed, looking closely at the chemical apparatus. There was a whole network of beakers and tubes bubbling merrily—and mysteriously.

"Hey, Leo!" Don called from the professor's computer station. "Look at this. There was some kind of fight here," he said, pointing to an overturned chair and a smashed glass beaker. Then they looked at the computer screen.

"What do you make of it, Donnie?" Leo asked.

Don scratched his head in thought. "Looks like

just a bunch of serial numbers. Look, it says 'Disposed. Disposed. Disposed . . .'"

"Hey, dudes," Michaelangelo said. They all turned to see what he'd found. It was a bin filled with completely empty canisters. And every one of them was identical to the canister Splinter had shown them!

"Like, no deposit, no return," Mike joked.

"Except maybe one," Don said, still looking at the computer screen.

"What do you mean?" Leo asked.

"Look." Leo pointed. There, on the screen, one serial number *didn't* say "Disposed." It said "Active"!

"Can you find where it is?" Leo asked.

"Well, I could try," Don said. "But if the database is coded, the system might go down."

It was a risk worth taking. "*Do it,*" Raph said. Don began.

He worked furiously, pounding away at the computer keyboard. His three brothers gathered behind him and watched. Don was simply a genius with machines of all kinds. They knew that if it could be done, he'd do it.

They were watching so intently that they never noticed the shadows on the wall behind them. They never heard the near-silent footsteps of approaching attackers. Only Don, spotting a strange flickering reflected on the computer screen, realized that a hand was being raised in attack.

"Look out!" he cried.

The four Turtles hit the floor so fast that Tatsu's

wrist crossbow fired uselessly at the screen, smashing it to smithereens.

Leo glanced out from behind the desk. He couldn't see much, but he could see enough.

"The Foot!" he said.

Don looked on the other side. What he saw was Tatsu—and there was something in his hand.

"The missing canister—he's got it!"

"Get it!" Raph yelled.

The Turtles attacked.

As they appeared from behind the desk and headed for Tatsu, their target tossed the canister to one of The Foot. This was a job for somebody really athletic. Mike sprang into the air, executed two back flips, and intercepted the pass.

"Ah-*ha*!"

He was trounced on by a swarm of black-garbed Foot.

"Ah-haaaugh!" he said in the middle of his sacking.

The canister flew into the air. One by one, green hands grabbed for it unsuccessfully. Black-gloved fingers grasped it, and the next thing the Turtles heard were the words "Ninja! Vanish!"

The room was filled with smoke from ninja smoke bombs, but not with ninja. They were gone.

"Hey, they're getting away!" Raph said.

"Yo, duhhhhhhh," his brothers commented. They all scrambled to get to their feet and begin the chase. And then they all realized that it wasn't so much that

The Foot were getting away. It was that they had gotten away. They had vanished!

Shredder tossed the canister gently in his hand, as if he were weighing it, testing its value.

"And this was the only one?" he asked.

"Ngghhh," Tatsu assured him.

"Then it's time to find out exactly what this ooze can do. Isn't it, Professor?"

He turned. Professor Perry sat in a chair nearby, still wearing his T.G.R.I. jumpsuit. That wasn't all he was wearing. He was also completely tied up with rope and he had a gag in his mouth.

11 =======

April was definitely having a hard time making up her mind how she felt. For one thing, the Turtles were just about her best friends and being with them was always interesting. Most of the time it was a lot of fun. Sometimes it was downright dangerous. On the other hand, they weren't the neatest roommates.

Michaelangelo removed his swimsuit calendar from the wall and rolled it up.

"But you guys haven't even found another place to live yet."

Leonardo shoved his belongings into a gym bag. "April, it's just too dangerous to stay here with you when The Foot are out there. They might be looking for us." None of them could forget what happened the last time The Foot had discovered the Turtles' hideout at April's apartment. The whole building had been burned down!

"Well, you know," Raph reasoned. "We could go

looking for *them* for a change. I mean, they got the ooze stuff—"

"First we move. Then we look," Donatello said sensibly.

Mike's mind was somewhere else—the same place it usually was. "Well, I don't know about you guys, but I could really go for some—"

"Pizza!" a voice called out from the hallway.

"Whoa, spookular!" Michaelangelo said, definitely surprised. Sometimes, his brothers could read his mind, especially when it came to pizza, but this was weird. "Hey, I didn't order any," he said, suspiciously.

Something pushed at the door. "Miss O'Neil?" a voice asked. It was a familiar voice. The Turtles couldn't place it, though. And they certainly didn't want *it* to place them!

"No, wait," April said, lodging her foot in front of the door.

In an instant the Turtles vanished—as much as a Turtle can actually vanish. Michaelangelo dropped on all fours and pulled a sheet over himself: instant table. Raph made himself into a plant holder. Leo and Don dashed for the kitchen and the bathroom. All of them heard the delivery boy enter the apartment before April let him in.

"What's up?" asked the delivery boy.

April glanced back over her shoulder, afraid of what she might see, but there was nothing telltale, just a very odd plant holder and a table with a wrinkled tablecloth on it.

"Uh, we, I mean, I didn't order any pizza," April said. "There must have been a mistake."

The delivery boy looked over April's shoulder, searching the apartment.

"I know, but the guy in 313 did, and now he doesn't seem to be there and I figured, since you order so much anyway, that maybe, you know . . ."

Then the Turtles realized why they recognized the voice. It was the delivery boy from the alley by the electronics store.

"Hmmm," Keno said, looking around. His eyes lit on Michaelangelo's nunchakus. "Where'd those come from?" he asked.

April thought fast. "They're mine," she said. She picked them up and began swinging them clumsily. "Yeah, I like to do a little 'chukking' every now and then."

She hit herself with the weapon.

"I'd keep practicing if I were you," Keno said.

He put the pizza down on the "table" and began to examine the plant holder. April was afraid he was onto something. She wanted him to leave.

"Well, you know, why don't I just take the pizza anyway?" She dropped the nunchakus on the floor before she did any more damage to herself. "Let me just get my wallet."

"No, no that's okay," Keno said, satisfied with his discoveries. "My mistake. One last thing, though . . ."

He lifted his right foot and stomped down on the base of the plant holder with his heel as hard as he could.

Raphael couldn't contain himself. "Yeooooooo!" he shrieked. The potted plant crashed to the floor and Raph hopped around on one foot—his good one.

"I *knew* it!" Keno declared.

Turtles began appearing from the most unlikely places.

"Can I hurt him?" Raph asked April, still groaning in agony. "Please? *Please* tell me I can hurt him!"

Keno just grinned. He felt pretty clever to have brought the odd creatures out of hiding—until he saw the oddest creature of all, a four-foot-tall rat. His jaw dropped.

"I think you'd better sit down," Splinter said. Keno sat down—right on the potted plant.

Although Splinter believed that the Turtles must always be invisible to the outside world, he knew that there were times when it was impossible. And when those times arose, he shared the story of the Turtles' beginnings. He told about the radioactive ooze that covered them as well as himself, their startling mutations, the way they all learned to talk, and the way he named the Turtles he'd come to think of as his children.

". . . and with an old Renaissance art book I found in a storm drain, I gave them all names." Then, one by one, he introduced the Turtles to Keno. "Leonardo, Michaelangelo, Donatello, and Raphael."

"Yeah, and all the good ones end in *o*," Mike teased.

Splinter stopped Raph from pushing his brother. Then he turned to Mike.

"Michaelangelo," he said sternly.

Mike knew what that meant. Without a word, Mike began doing flips. "One . . . two . . ."

"So, basically, what you're telling me is that all you guys were slimed?" Keno said.

"It wasn't slime. It was ooze," Raph said. He was still upset about his foot.

"And there's more of it out there," Leonardo told Keno.

"Where?" Keno asked.

"Five . . . six . . ." They could hear Michaelangelo counting. He grunted as he worked out.

"We're not sure," Don answered. "See, there's this sort of 'clan' of ninja thieves, a really secret group that call themselves—"

"The Foot?" Keno supplied.

"You've heard of them?" Don said, surprised.

Keno nodded. "Well, see, word on the street is that there are these guys looking for anybody they can find with martial arts talent, especially teenagers. Hey, I've got an idea. I could let myself get 'recruited,' and guess what that might lead us to!"

"Big trouble," April said.

"No way, Keno," Leo said. "Forget about it."

Raph wasn't so sure, though. "Hey, and believe me, I really hate to say this, but the kid's got a—"

"No," Splinter said.

"Fourteen . . . fifteen." Michaelangelo droned away in the background.

"Why not?" Raphael and Keno asked at the same instant.

"Too dangerous," Splinter said.

"But . . ." Raph tried.

"No," Splinter said, closing the subject. Annoyed, Raph stormed out of the room.

"Seventeen . . . eighteen . . ." Michaelangelo grunted again. Splinter, April, Keno, Don, and Leo turned to watch him finish his stint of twenty. What they saw was Mike standing in the corner, doing excellent sound effects. "Nineteen . . . unh . . . twenty."

The sudden quiet made him look up. He wasn't expecting an audience. He blushed. "Uh-oh," he said. "Just taking a break, see. I'll start where I left off—at, uh, fifteen?"

"One," Splinter said.

"Yes, Master," Mike said. Then, good-naturedly, he began at the beginning.

"One . . . two . . ."

12

In the small building in the junkyard, Shredder, Tatsu, and several Foot watched intently while Professor Jordan Perry worked. He had used discarded containers and tubing from the junkyard to make his chemical setup. There was a rubber hose leading from one of the pots, across the ceiling of the shack, and into a couple of small barred holding cells. Shredder looked at the cells and then at Tatsu.

"Those were the two most vicious animals you could find at night?"

"Ngggh," Tatsu confirmed.

"Good," Shredder said. Then he turned to the scientist at work. "Professor?" he asked.

"Preparations are complete. However . . ."

"Begin," Shredder said, uninterested in the professor's hesitation.

"However," the professor continued, not wanting to be interrupted, "I feel compelled to reregister my formal protest and remind you of the imminent dangers of . . ."

He was interrupted. He was interrupted by Tatsu, who glared at him threateningly. Professor Perry knew when a battle was lost. "But enough talk," he said lightly. "Let's begin."

He turned a valve on his setup, raising a flame beneath a pot. The greenish liquid began to bubble menacingly. It swelled and rose, spurting through the tubing and, finally, into the holding pens, where it sprayed with tremendous pressure.

Beneath his mask, Shredder grinned in anticipation.

13

April stood alone in the middle of the street. She tried to look natural. It wasn't easy. She was standing there, over an open manhole, with an umbrella in her hand, glancing up and down the street furtively.

"Clear!" she whispered toward the shadow of the entrance to her own apartment building.

A green blur passed her. "See you, April." Leonardo disappeared into the sewer.

"Wish us luck!" the Raphael blur said, following his brother into the hole.

"We'll be back for Splinter!" Donatello said, sliding into the darkness after Raphael.

Michaelangelo wasn't in such a hurry. He knew an opportunity for one of his famous impressions when he saw one. He turned up the collar of his trench coat, pulled down the brim of his hat, and became Humphrey Bogart.

"I know the lives of two people don't amount to

a hill of beans in this crazy world, Ilsa, but that's why you're getting on that plane." April could almost feel the hot winds of the North African desert whip past her, instead of the cold rain of New York. "Maybe not today, maybe not tomorrow, but soon . . ." For a Turtle, Michaelangelo sounded an awful lot like Rick in *Casablanca*. " . . . and for the rest of your—"

A green hand reached up from the manhole and grabbed Mike by the ankle. Before he could finish the teary farewell, he was gone!

April giggled. She loved Mike's impressions.

Above the Turtles, the manhole cover clunked into place. They were back in the sewers of New York and they were in the market for a place to call home.

"All right, hold it," Raph said, more than a little annoyed. He couldn't help thinking there was something more to be done than looking for someplace to live. "This is *stupid*. We got The Foot up there, with the ooze, and we're down here, playing Century 21!"

"Ra-aph," Leonardo said. He was exasperated.

"Come on, Leo," Raph countered. "Even *you* could think of something better to do than this."

He certainly could, but if Splinter were around, it would have cost him twenty flips. He glared instead.

"That's it. I'm out of here," Raph announced, looking for a ladder to climb to the street.

"No, you're not," Leo said. He grabbed Raph's arm.

"Let go!"

They were about to get into a fight when Mike intervened with another one of his impressions. This time, instead of Humphrey Bogart, he was a hard-sell real-estate man on late-night television. "I have the answer to all your housing needs: *time-share!*"

Raph relaxed a little. Leo smiled. Donatello put a hand on Mike's head, as if he were testing melons at the market.

"Not quite ripe yet," he announced.

Mike's antics stopped a fight, but they didn't stop Raphael's determination to do something other than house hunting. "I'm gone," he said. He turned and left.

Raphael could be moody, and there was no way to change that. His brothers knew they couldn't convince him to stick with them. He'd do what he wanted to do and he'd be back with them eventually. In the meantime, they had a job to do.

Leo led the way.

"You know," Don said, glancing around for a hint of a place to settle down, "you'd think finding a new place would be easy. . . ."

"But noooooo. . . ." Mike continued for him.

"You'd think even an *idiot* could find a place down here. . . ."

"But noooooo. . . ."

"You'd think—"

"Oooooaaaahhhhhhh!"

Leo and Don turned around to see what had happened to Mike, but there was no sign of him. Only sounds.

"Yaaaoooooooouuuuh!"

"Mike? Mike! Are you okay?"

No answer.

"Mike?!"

"Check it *out*!" came Mike's excited reply.

Leo and Don followed Mike's voice. They found themselves standing over a hole where the floor had caved in.

"Come on down!" Mike invited them, "The Price Is Right" style. They did.

When they got to solid ground, they were standing in the middle of an abandoned subway station, sectioned off by caved-in rubble. It even had an old subway car.

"Well, I'll be," Donatello began.

"It's well hidden," Leo reasoned.

"Roomy," Don said. "And it's got access to power and water. What do you think, Mike?"

"Maybe it's time for a move to suburbia?"

"Home, sweet home," Leo cooed. The decision was made.

14

"**H**ow much longer?" Shredder demanded.

"I told you, I don't know. It takes time, days," Professor Perry answered. It wasn't what Shredder wanted to hear.

Shredder crossed the room to the holding cells and glanced in. "I want them as soon as possible," he said.

"I *told* you—" He was ready to give Shredder a piece of his mind. Instead, three of The Foot grabbed the professor, shoving him back into his chair. "Aren't *these* enough for you?" the professor asked Shredder angrily, pointing to the black-clad men who were guarding him.

"The Foot have already failed against my enemies," he said, hatred dripping from every word. "I have failed." He walked back over to the cages. "But the next time will be different," he pledged. "The next time will be freak against freak!"

There was sudden activity in the cage. One of the animals snarled and snapped at Shredder's shadow. The other growled loudly and began banging angrily at the bars on the cage.

Shredder permitted a smile to cross his face.

15

Whenever Raph decided to disobey Splinter, he didn't go halfway. He went the whole way. He was convinced he was right. He was convinced that getting Keno into The Foot was the best way to defeat Shredder.

Raph stood in the shadow of an alley, watching, waiting. Nearby, a tough-looking teenager was talking to a group of young men. One of those young men was Keno.

". . . so everybody's got to take a little test," the tough kid explained. "*Then,* if you're good enough, we let you in the 'organization.' Any questions?"

There were none. The young men followed their leader. Keno held back. He wanted to talk to Raph.

"I *knew* this would work," the new recruit said eagerly.

"Just remember," Raph said. "We get you in, we find the Foot headquarters, we get out and tell the others, right?"

"Gee, maybe I should write this down," Keno mocked. Then, before Raph could answer, he ran after the group.

Raph looked up at the sky. "I'm being punished, aren't I?" He didn't wait for an answer. He trailed after Keno, out of sight, but, he hoped, still in Keno's mind.

The recruiter took the boys to a warehouse, where he put them through tests of their martial arts skills. Most of the boys weren't very good. The recruiter excused them one by one. With Keno it was different. Keno repelled the Foot attack easily with a series of deft ninja moves. Within seconds, three Foot lay on the mat. Keno was still standing. The recruiter was definitely impressed.

" 'Keno,' was it? You seem to be the only one worthy of a final test," he said. Keno had the feeling it was going to be a tough one.

He was right. The recruiter showed him a mannequin completely covered with tiny bells.

"You'll have fifteen seconds," the recruiter said. "Remove as many bells as you can. One sound, and you fail."

Keno figured the only way he could avoid making a sound would be to head for the exit!

"Oh, and one other thing," the recruiter added. He pulled a ninja dust bomb from his pocket and dropped it on the floor. It exploded. "We work in concealment. Fifteen seconds. Go."

Keno was surrounded by dust. He found that he was also surrounded by a whirling cloud of green. Raphael to the rescue!

When the fifteen seconds were done and the smoke had settled, the recruiter found Keno, his arms cradling all the bells and the dummy—completely stripped.

"Is this enough?" Keno asked smugly.

The recruiter just nodded. He couldn't speak.

16

The old subway station was beginning to look like home for the Turtles and Splinter. At least that was the case for three of the Turtles. There had been no sign of Raphael since he'd stormed out of the sewer.

His brothers had checked the logical places, the old Foot headquarters, the T.G.R.I. waste site and lab, but there was nothing there. "Zip-o-lady, dudes," as Michaelangelo put it, speaking for all of them.

There was nothing to do but wait. In the meantime, they worked on their living quarters. Donatello was trying to fix the television. It wasn't easy to get good reception in a subway station. So far, all he could see was fuzz and all he could hear was buzz. Mike was setting up a place where they could eat—pizza, of course—and Leo was cleaning up debris.

Their work was interrupted by footsteps above and then the arrival of . . . "April!" Don said. He recognized her legs coming down the rope ladder.

"What brings you here?" Leo asked. He took her coat and found a rock to hang it on.

"Well, I'm not sure," April said. "But I think I found out some news about T.G.R.I."

Splinter bowed to her respectfully. "Our puzzle is far from complete. Any new piece would be welcome," he said solemnly.

"Well, I was doing a report there this morning, trying to get some more information, and I noticed a lot of equipment being moved out. They seemed a little short on employees, too."

The Turtles and Splinter were very interested.

"I think they're shutting down," April said.

Then the buzz of the television stopped abruptly. "Hey, I got it!" Don announced proudly. The others looked at the screen, now showing a very clear picture of none other than April O'Neil!

"But why has T.G.R.I. been avoiding my follow-up calls?" she asked the camera.

"I'm not a spokesman, Miss O'Neil," a uniformed T.G.R.I. employee told her. "I'm just trying to get to work."

April watched herself on the screen. "I couldn't get much out of these guys," she said.

On the television, April persisted, following one of T.G.R.I.'s assistants to the door of the building. "But what about possible genetic abnormalities?" she asked. "Mutants?"

The assistant stopped and turned to the camera. "There's far more science fiction than science in questions like that, Miss O'Neil," he said. He seemed to be mocking her. "Mutants, indeed." He smirked and entered the building.

In the subway tunnel, four mutants looked at one human being. There was work to be done. Definitely.

17

The holding cells rocked and rattled. The two mutant creatures had become so large that they nearly burst the steel-reinforced cages.

"Their cells will no longer hold them," Shredder said. He loved the vicious sounds the animals made, too.

"Nggh," Tatsu agreed.

"Let them out," Shredder commanded.

"Nggh?" Tatsu asked.

Shredder nodded. "It's time they learned who their master is."

"Ngghhh. . . ." Tatsu said doubtfully.

"Remove the bar. And leave us."

Tatsu hesitated, but he did as he'd been ordered. The art of ninja had taught him to move quickly. As soon as he'd opened the cages, he fled from the room, closing the door behind him.

"Come forth!" Shredder commanded the mutants.

The first creature to step out had once been a wolf. Now it was a gigantic snarling, growling, roaring mutant canine. Saliva dripped menacingly from its bared teeth. Shredder smiled coldly. He named it Rahzar.

Then came the other mutant. It had been born a snapping turtle. Now, it was a great deal more. For one thing, it was enormous. It opened its mouth, seeking something to bite. Even Shredder was impressed by the span of its jaw. When the mutant snapped its mouth shut, Shredder could imagine Turtles and rats meeting their doom. His eyes gleamed with pleasure. He named the snapping turtle Tokka.

"Incredible," Shredder said. The animals stepped toward him. He spoke to them. "Yes, come forward," he invited them. "Attack if you will. But when it is over you *will* call me 'master.'"

The animals stopped suddenly.

"Ma . . . ma . . ." Rahzar said, trying to repeat the last word Shredder had said.

Tokka tried then, too. "Mama?" he asked.

Shredder was not pleased.

"Mama, mama," Tokka repeated. Razhar did the same. Their young mouths had trouble with the syllables, but they each seemed pleased to have accomplished their first words.

Shredder was very *dis*pleased.

"Babies! They're babies!" Shredder roared, bursting through the door to the shack. In anger, he picked up everything in his path and threw it helter-skelter all over the place. He was furious.

When he finally returned to the shack, he found his two mutant babies playing on the floor of the building. Rahzar sat willingly while the professor examined him. Nearby on the floor, Tokka had a length of six-inch-diameter pipe. He played with it like a kitten would play with a string.

Professor Perry faced Shredder's fury with a shrug. "Well, what did you expect? Thought they'd come out quoting Shakespeare?"

Shredder didn't try to hide his disdain. "They're *stupid*!" he said.

The professor shook his head. "They're not stupid," he contradicted Shredder. "They're infants."

"Okay, then, they're stupid infants," Shredder conceded.

Just then Tokka picked up the pipe and bit it into two pieces. Even in a "stupid infant," it was an impressive, and frightening, display.

"Put that down!" Shredder said sharply. Without hesitation, Tokka put the pipe back on the floor and lowered his head as if he were ashamed of himself.

"Fortunately they seem to have decided you are their mother and they want to obey you."

It didn't seem like much consolation to Shredder. "They are of no use to me like this. Tatsu, see that these two 'things' are destroyed!"

Tatsu signaled the mutants to leave the shack.

"No! You can't do that!" Professor Perry said. "They're living things!"

"Not for long," Shredder told him.

The creatures followed Tatsu out to the junkyard.

The professor couldn't believe that Shredder would just destroy his experiment! "Wait! Yes, they may be intellectually inferior," he said. "But . . ."

Shredder was looking out the window. The professor joined him. They both saw that the mutants had started playing a game of keepaway, with Tatsu in between them. What made it different from other games of keepaway was that what they were tossing around was a seven-hundred-pound engine block!

"Hmmm," Shredder said thoughtfully. "Maybe I'll keep them around after all."

18 ═══════

Raphael was still trailing Keno and the recruiter invisibly when they got to Foot headquartes. Raph could hardly believe what a dump it was. Literally. It seemed to be an endless junkyard, piled high with scrap metal. The only building was a little shack.

The recruiter pointed to the shack. "Get yourself a training *dogi*," he told Keno. "And meet me in the yard."

Keno ran off to the shack. Raphael ran alongside him, dodging behind piles of scrap to remain invisible.

"Okay, first chance we get, we're out of here," Raph said. He didn't want to risk one second more than necessary with The Foot. They had the information they needed. The next trick would be to make a swift—and safe—exit.

Then something in the shack caught Raphael's eye. He could have sworn it was ninja armor. He'd only seen ninja armor like that one time before. He thought he'd seen it for the last time, too!

"What is it?" Keno asked.

Raph didn't know, but he was afraid he'd just seen a ghost. He ducked behind a pile of debris and approached the shack, sneaking up to one of the windows.

"Just what are you looking for, anyway?" Keno asked.

Raphael put a finger to his lips. "Quiet," he whispered. "Do you want to get us—"

It was too late.

"—caught?" Raph turned around and found himself facing Tatsu and several Foot. He decided to try evasive action. "Uh, hi, guys," he said casually. "We were looking for a muffler for a seventy-seven Chevy?"

"Nggggh," Tatsu said. Raph didn't understand the word, but he got the message and it wasn't good.

Tatsu and his band attacked Raph at once. Raph knew there was only one course of action to take. He held them off as well as he could and kept them away from Keno.

"Get out of here!" he said to the boy. "Tell the others! Go! Now!"

Keno hesitated for a second and then hit the road, running as fast as he could.

Raph was good, but not that good. He could keep a few ninja warriors out of the way long enough to save Keno, but there wasn't much he could do for himself against Tatsu and fifteen fighters.

"I'm curious," he tried. "Have any of you guys ever heard the expression 'fair fight'?" Apparently

they hadn't. Very quickly he was completely immobilized by the entire squadron. Tatsu stood in front of him and grunted his satisfaction.

"You know, pal," Raphael said to Tatsu. "If I had a face like yours, I'd try to make up for it with some sort of personality." It didn't win Tatsu over. He just threatened Raph. Raph thought his only chance would be if the men who held him let him go so he could fight Tatsu one-on-one. He wanted to bait the grunting ninja warrior and was about to start in on him again when he saw something that made him silent.

He saw shining ninja armor, a black cape, and a razor-studded hood.

"Shredder!" he said.

It didn't take long for Tatsu to completely subdue Raphael. Tatsu entered the shack and reported to Shredder.

"Captured Turtle now secure," he grunted.

"Good. An unexpected advantage. And the boy?"

Tatsu lowered his head in shame. "Gone," he confessed.

"Also good," Shredder said, surprising Tatsu. "Now, all we have to do is wait."

Tatsu understood then.

19

Leonardo, Donatello, and Michaelangelo peered down at the junkyard from their perch on a huge pile of scrap metal.

"Just like Keno said it was," Mike remarked.

Donatello glanced around. "The perimeter's quiet."

"Yeah, a little *too* quiet," Leo said skeptically.

They crept down the pile and into the junkyard. They were in.

"Well, that was easy," Donatello said.

"Yeah, a little *too* easy," Leonardo said skeptically.

Donatello squinted to see through the dimness. There, at the far end of the junkyard, tied to a stake, was his brother.

"Look, it's Raph!"

"Yeah, a little *too* Raph," Michaelangelo said, imitating Leo.

"Knock it off. Keep your eyes peeled. I don't like

this." Leonardo didn't have to say it twice. They crept forward soundlessly.

They were about twenty yards from Raphael and still creeping forward when Donatello spoke.

"You know, given the layout of this junkyard and the proximity of certain structures, if they *were* going to spring a trap, they'd probably do it right about—"

Floodlights flashed. Something snapped. Suddenly, all three rescuers were whisked upward in a large net. They were trapped and suspended from a crane.

"Here," Donatello finished.

"Nice call, Donnie," Michaelangelo said sarcastically. "Pitifully *late,* but nice."

They looked down and saw a crowd of Foot men nearby. The crowd parted, making room for someone to pass through. The Turtles couldn't believe their eyes.

"The *Shred*-dude!" Michaelangelo said.

"I've been waiting for you," Shredder said. "And I have a little surprise for you."

He gave a signal and the ground in front of Raphael rose, revealing razor-sharp ninja spikes. Their crane swung around. They were headed right for the spikes!

"Uh-oh. Turtle kabobs!" Michaelangelo said.

The Turtles struggled against their bonds, trying to rip the net, trying to have a chance.

"You know, these nets are remarkably well constructed," Donatello observed. It was just like him to admire someone else's technical ability, even when he was on the verge of being shredded by it!

"Yeah, remind me to drop a note to Ralph Nader!"

But the only thing that was dropping was the Turtles themselves!

Splinter stood on a mound of junk a hundred yards away. Slowly and carefully he raised his ninja crossbow and aimed. The arrow whizzed from his weapon. It slashed through the rope that held the Turtles' net and it stuck in the stake above Raphael's head.

"Cowabunga!" Splinter said, utterly pleased with himself.

Leo, Mike, and Don fell to the ground. They weren't hurt at all. They got themselves ready to fight. "Hey, Shredder—you forgot that we carry insurance," Leo said.

"Mutual of Splinter, dude!" Michaelangelo said.

Shredder was in no mood for jokes. "Get them!" he commanded.

The Foot tried, but they were no match for the Turtles. Within seconds, the half-shelled Turtles had The Foot on the run. Don and Mike freed Raphael and that increased their Turtle power even more. The Turtles were about ready to exchange high threes and head for the sewers when they heard Shredder say something very odd.

"Tokka! Razhar!" he cried.

And with those words, the walls of the junkyard shack came crashing down.

Leonardo couldn't believe how big and mean the creatures were. "What the—?" he asked.

"Didn't I see these guys on Wrestlemania?" Mike joked.

But it was no joke. The mutants attacked the Turtles.

Raph shrugged. "Well, you know what they say. The bigger they come—"

"The more bones they break?" Mike said.

Don squared off with Tokka. He held him back with his *bo*. Tokka bit it in two pieces. Tokka picked up Don and sent him flying through the air, past some junk, and the walls of a small toolshed. When he opened his eyes, he was looking right at Professor Perry, bound and gagged.

"Hey, you're the T.G.R.I. guy!"

"Mmmphhhughrrauuu," he said through the tape.

Don realized the problem right away. He grabbed a corner of the tape and ripped it off. He took off some of the professor's skin, too!

"Yeouuuuchhhh!" the professor remarked.

There was no time for apologies. Don untied the professor and the two of them got back to where the other Turtles were still fighting the mutants. Rahzar and Tokka weren't skilled fighters like the Turtles, but they were big and they were mean. It looked as if that could be enough.

"We can't keep this up much longer!" Leo said desperately.

Michaelangelo flew past him, another victim of Tokka's playful tosses. He landed with a loud clunk on something hard and metal. It was a manhole cover.

"Am I glad to see you!" he said. If he and his brothers could get into the sewer, then they'd be on their way home! He called to his brothers. "Guys! Over here!" he yelled. He removed the manhole cover. The first to arrive were Don and the professor. They climbed right down into the sewer.

"Way to go, Mikie!" Raphael said, fighting Tokka and Rahzar with all his might. Mikie went. Soon Raph and Leo joined the others.

"No! Stop them!" Shredder cried.

Tokka didn't hesitate. He leapt right into the manhole, feet first. His feet were about all that got in there, too. He wedged himself tightly in the hole and he couldn't move an inch, up or down.

Shredder turned red with fury.

Tokka smiled up at the master he'd learned to call Mama. "Tokka stuck," he said sweetly.

20

Michaelangelo paused on the ladder into the sewer and looked up at the oversized form of Tokka. He couldn't resist. He reached up and tickled Tokka's feet. Tokka kicked and giggled. It was pretty weird.

"Come on," Leonardo said. "We've got to meet back up with Splinter."

But first, there was the professor. He stared at the foursome. "Four *turtles*!" he said, as if he'd just realized who rescued him.

"Yeah, the guy's Ph.D. material all right," Raph joked.

"And so intelligent! It's incredible," Professor Perry said.

"Hey, don't freak, dude, we can explain," Mike said. "See . . ."

The professor began speaking then. It was as if he knew what Mike was going to say. "Fifteen years ago, you came in contact with a green colloidal gel down in a sewer that transformed you to your present state."

The Turtles stared at him in disbelief.

"Fascinating," the professor said.

The Turtles thought it was definitely fascinating. There was a lot to talk about, but it would have to wait until they got back to their new home. Just to be on the safe side, they blindfolded the professor. They didn't want anybody to know the whereabouts of their den.

When the blindfold came off, the professor looked around at the reconstructed subway station.

"Ingenious," the professor said.

"We'll give you the tour later," Leo told him. "Right now we've got a few questions."

Splinter stepped out of the shadow. The professor's jaw dropped when he saw the rat. Splinter spoke then. "The professor has much to tell us."

It was true, too.

Once introductions had been made, the professor began talking. He explained about an experiment T.G.R.I. had been conducting fifteen years before.

". . . Of course, laboratories were crude back than and an accident was just waiting to happen."

"You mean to tell us that the formation of the ooze was all just a big mistake?" Don asked. He didn't like that idea. He preferred to think that he and his brothers had been planned.

"Well, you see, Donatello, an unknown mixture of discarded chemicals was accidentally exposed to a series of radiative waves. The resulting, uh, ooze, as

you call it, was found to have remarkable and dangerous mutagenic properties."

"Huh?" Mike asked, looking to Raph for an explanation.

"Big mistake," Raph translated.

"Well, on our way to bury it, a near-collision
caused us to lose one of the canisters down a sewer.
Fifteen years ago."

That was the answer. Now the Turtles and Splinter knew the real answer to their existence. They
were just one big mistake on top of another.

The professor excused himself then. He needed
a rest. The Turtles needed a rest, too. They were all
feeling let down.

"What troubles you, my son?" Splinter asked
Don, who seemed particularly low.

"I don't know," he said. "I just always thought
there'd be more to it. I thought we'd find out we
were special."

"Do not confuse the specter of your origin with
your present worth, my sons. The search for a beginning rarely has an easy end. For now, though, our
search will have to wait. Tonight's encounter has left
us with larger problems."

There were names for those problems: Rahzar
and Tokka.

21

By the next morning, Rahzar and Tokka had left a calling card for the Turtles. Shredder had let them loose on one of the city's streets. They'd had a ball! They knocked down signal lights and lampposts and they crushed cars.

April interviewed Police Chief Sterns. As usual, he didn't have much information to give. He didn't seem very interested in getting any, either.

". . . and, as always, our official report will be released after a thorough investigation," he told the camera. "Thank you, Miss O'Neil."

"More as it develops," April said. The camera clicked off.

April tossed her microphone to one of her assistants and followed the chief.

"I wonder if I might ask you a few more questions—off the record?"

He tried to ignore her and walk away. She persisted.

"Were there any large tooth and claw marks found here today?"

Chief Sterns stopped and turned. "How did you know?" Then he realized he'd said something he hadn't meant to say. "Uh, I mean that I don't know what you're talking about."

"Chief, I have reason to believe that this damage was caused by two, uh, really big animals."

"Oh? And what type of animals might these be, Miss O'Neil?" he asked suspiciously.

"Well, I can't say, exactly." April was uncomfortable. It seemed as if the chief were interviewing *her,* and she didn't want to tell him anything.

"I see," he said. "Then what leads you to believe they did this?"

"Well, I can't say that, either."

"Hmmm. Was there anything else you'd like 'not' to tell me, Miss O'Neil?"

Before April could give him another nonanswer, he turned and left her. April shook her head. These creatures weren't a problem the police could solve anyway. It was going to take special talent—and a lot of it, too!

April needed to talk to the Turtles. She hurried to finish the work so she could return to the studio. But when she opened the back door to the equipment van, she found more than equipment there. A black-gloved hand grabbed her from behind and covered her mouth. Someone dragged her into an alley.

Then somebody in a black ninja *dogi* and mask spoke.

"Hello, April," he said.

She knew the voice. It was Freddy, her assistant!

"Our master has a message for your 'friends,'" Freddy said. He leaned forward to whisper in her ear.

She heard every word.

22

The Turtles didn't want to believe what April was telling them, but they knew it was true.

". . . and they told me that if you don't go to this construction site tonight, Shredder's going to send Tokka and Rahzar out again—into Central Park."

"Central Park!? But how would they avoid hurting all those people?" Donatello asked. Then he realized that they *wouldn't* avoid hurting the people. A lot of people would get hurt. It would be much worse than a few lampposts.

"Then there is no choice but to meet as the Shredder wishes," Splinter said.

"There's no other way," Raphael agreed.

"But you don't have a chance!" April said, near tears.

"Wait." The professor spoke. Everybody turned to him. "There might be a way."

It was a busy afternoon. Professor Perry used Donatello as his chief lab assistant. The other Turtles and Keno watched the pair work, helping when they could. Together they managed to assemble a chemical apparatus of beakers, tubes, and burners.

"Temperature?" the professor asked.

Donatello checked the thermometer. "Three-thirty-eight, Kelvin," he said.

"Michaelangelo, hand me some more of the di-methylchlorinate."

Mike looked around at the collection of bottles. "Uhhh," he said.

"There." The professor pointed.

Mike picked up a bright pink liquid and passed it to the professor. "You know, not to criticize science or anything, but wouldn't it be better just to call it the pink one?"

The professor poured some of the pink liquid into the vat that was bubbling merrily on the fire—at 338 Kelvin.

"Donatello, continue aeration."

Donatello took an egg beater, inserted it into the glop, and proceeded with "aeration."

Raphael peered into the vat and made a face. It smelled terrible. "You sure this stuff will work?" he asked the professor.

"When I contaminated the ooze used to transform Tokka and Rahzar, making them intellectually inferior and, thus, less dangerous, I had no idea I'd later be trying to formulate an antimutagen based on that contamination."

"Huh?" said Mike. If being able to say things other people didn't understand meant somebody was smart, he thought the professor must be a real genius!

"It means he's not sure," Raphael translated.

"See, we won't know until we actually spray those guys," Donatello explained.

The professor cleared his throat. "Uh, actually," he began. "I'm afraid ingestion is the only course."

"Wha?" Leo, Raph, Don, and Keno asked in a single voice.

Michaelangelo understood. "You meant they have to *eat* it?" he asked.

"Affirma—I mean, uh, *yo,* my man," he said. He was learning Turtle talk.

Leo sniffed the vile mixture. He made a face. "Uh, that'll be easy. We can put it on some pizza," he joked. It wasn't a joke, though. The stuff smelled so bad, nobody would ever eat it voluntarily.

"Well, I've got an idea," Mike said.

23

The Turtles were on time for their "invitation" from Shredder. They were to meet at a skyscraper construction site right by the East River. They were armed and skilled, but they were worried. There were a lot of "ifs" in their plan.

"Do you think it will work?" Don asked Mike about his crazy scheme.

"Is, like, Schwarzenegger hard to spell?" Mike answered. Mike's confidence helped. Now, if only his plan would work as well. . . .

Everything was dark and quiet at the construction site. Too quiet.

"Shredder!!!" Raph howled.

Don was so startled that he jumped a foot and a half. "Gee, thanks, Raph. I may never have hiccups again!"

Then the lights went on and Shredder appeared.

"Welcome," he said. The Turtles had the awful feeling he really meant it. He was glad to see them and it wasn't because he was going to give them dinner. They were going to *be* dinner for Tokka and Rahzar!

The Foot stood in a circle, surrounding the Turtles and Shredder's mutants.

"Let the games begin!" Shredder commanded.

It was the moment of truth. "Wait!" Leonardo said, as Mike had cued him. "First, we should observe the ancient ritual of—well, the traditional, you know, prefight doughnut."

Before Shredder could object, Mike and Leo hurried toward the eager mutants with a box of doughnuts. Tokka and Rahzar each downed a doughnut and licked their chops. They loved them! Rahzar grabbed another treat, but he was so strong that he mangled the doughnut and the anti-mutagen cube popped out. Rahzar looked at it curiously. Shredder, however, wasn't curious; he was furious.

"Kill them!" Shredder commanded. Tokka and Rahzar set about to do just that.

"The stuff's not working!" Leo said while Tokka did his best to squeeze all the air out of him.

"Maybe we should have brought muffins?" Mike suggested.

Before he could crack another joke, both Mike and Leo were flying across the construction site. They landed right on top of their brothers. The four of them tumbled in a clump.

"Now I know what a postal package feels like," Mike joked weakly.

"Plan B?" Leo suggested.

"Oh, no," Raph said sarcastically. "Let's try that doughnut thing again." He glared at Michaelangelo.

Leo took the lead. "Weapons!" he cried, urging his brothers back to the battle.

"Hey, wait, look!" Don said.

They all looked at Tokka and Rahzar. The mutants seemed decidedly uncomfortable.

"The antimutagen! It's working!" Don declared excitedly.

"Yeah, about time!" Raph remarked.

The two creatures stood erect. They had sour looks on their faces. And then at exactly the same time, they both did exactly the same thing.

"UUUUURRRP!" They burped.

Now, much more comfortable, they started snarling and snapping at the Turtles. The real attack was about to begin.

"Wow, man. Ugly and impolite," Mike remarked.

"Now what?" Raph asked Leo.

Leo reached for his weapons. "Improvise!" he told his brother.

And that's just what Tokka and Rahzar did, too. Tokka used Mike as a baseball and tried a little fungo. Mike was smashed against the wall of a nearby rock 'n' roll club. Mike learned the name of the place when he crashed through the sign. It was the Dockside Club.

Rahzar was a football fan. He practiced drop kicks with Leo and Raph. They flew right *through* the wall next to Mike and into the Dockside Club, interrupting a rapper.

One of the customers saw the Turtles and thought they were part of the act. He started cheering. "Man, check out those costumes! I love this place!"

Leo and Raph looked around, still wondering exactly how they'd made it through the wall.

"I think we're wearing them down," Raph said weakly to Leo.

Tokka looked very rested when he stormed into the club after his prey.

"Yeah, definitely," Leo said.

Michaelangelo and Donatello flew in then, landing next to Leo. The first thing Mike noticed was the music, which hadn't stopped.

"Hey, check it out! This place is rocking!"

"Great. Now we can get pulverized to a beat!"

The audience seemed to think it was great, too.

Chairs began flying. The audience went wild.

Don spotted the professor, who had come to see the end of his experiment. The two of them took cover behind the bar.

"It would appear the antimutagen has been somewhat ineffective," the professor understated.

Out on the dance floor, Leo and Raph tried to fend off Tokka, who simply snapped everything in his way with his teeth.

"Well, there is one bright side to this," Leo said. "It can't get worse."

As if on cue, Tatsu and hundreds of Foot began pouring into the club.

"You know, Leo, you should get a job on Wall Street," Raph said.

Behind the bar the professor and Don talked about the situation. Don told him about the burps.

"Hmm, very bad. Carbon dioxide is essential to

the process. When they burped, they slowed the whole thing down."

"Isn't there any way we can speed it up?" Don asked.

"We have to reintroduce carbon dioxide. The problem is finding a ready supply."

The two scientists looked around them for an answer—and there it was. The bar had a full shelf of old-fashioned seltzer bottles. That meant an almost unlimited supply of carbon dioxide!

Within a few minutes the Turtles were ready and armed with squirting seltzer bottles.

"You sure about this, Donnie?" Leo asked.

"Just do it!" Don insisted. "Now!"

Mike was game for anything. "Bonzaiiiiii!" he said, and rushed into the fray. Raph was by his side. On Don's signal, they each bashed into one of the mutants' stomachs. Tokka and Rahzar were momentarily stunned. That caused them to drop their jaws. That, in turn, caused Don and Leo to spray seltzer down their throats. And that caused Tokka and Rahzar to roar furiously when they'd recovered.

"What now, Donnie?" Leo asked. "Beer nuts?"

"I don't get it. It should have worked. . . ."

Suddenly Tokka grasped his stomach. Rahzar paled and clutched his stomach, too.

"Tummy," Rahzar said.

"Ache." Tokka finished the thought.

And with that, they both konked out and toppled over—right onto Michaelangelo. He squeezed out from under the unconscious monsters. "These dudes

are copping major z's," he observed, though it was hard to hear him for all the applause from the audience, to say nothing of the mutants' snoring!

"Good," Leo said. "Now let's have some fun!"

The four Turtles turned to face their old enemy, The Foot. It seemed as if the whole club had been filled with energy. The four Turtles were fighting as one against a teeming mass of The Foot Clan—all to the beat of a rap performer on the stage.

The audience stood and cheered wildly, stomping on the ground with the tempo of the music. It was just the rhythm the Turtles needed. They were ready to beat The Foot with the beat of the feet.

"Cowabunga!" Mike cried, dispensing with two Foot at once.

"C-C-C-Cowabunga, Cowa-Cowa-bunga!" His words echoed back from the tape deck onstage.

Then the rap singer got into the swing of it all:

> *"Well, it looks kinda weird,*
> *But it's plain to be seen,*
> *The bad guys wear black,*
> *And the good guys be green!"*

Flashbulbs went off, the audience shrieked with the beat, and the last Foot met defeat. Finally, there was only Tatsu. The Turtles finished him off and howled a triumphant "Ninja Rap!" when they were done.

Mike turned to the audience. "If you liked what you saw, ladies and gentlemen, give it up for the Turtles! Come on, give it up!" They roared approval in a chorus of "Uh-uh-uhs." They waved their arms while they cheered.

Then Raph held up both hands. "Show's over, folks. Show's over."

But it wasn't. For just then a long, dark shadow appeared on the stage, and then the creature that had cast it: Shredder.

"We're not through yet," he said. "The battle is yours. But the war is far from over. Not so long as I possess—*this!*"

He held a familiar, and deadly, green canister in his hands.

There was a stunned silence. Then somebody in the audience turned to his date. "Can you believe it? Music *and* a play? Want to come back *next* Friday?"

The Turtles circled Shredder and prepared for attack. Just as Leo was about to give the signal, there was a ninja howl from the rear of the audience. Keno had arrived! He raced through the crowd and leapt onto the stage.

That made two things happen. It startled Shredder so that he dropped the canister. The canister fell to the dance area and skittered across the floor, coming to a halt at the professor's feet.

He picked it up and saluted the Turtles. "Farewell, my friends," he said, and disappeared through the door.

The other thing that happened was that Keno kept going until he ran smack into Shredder. Shredder grabbed him and he became Shredder's hostage before the Turtles could move to attack.

Shredder threatened Keno with his razor-sharp

armor. The audience booed. Shredder stood in front of a large amplifier, which protected his flank.

"You're not going anywhere, Shredder," Raphael said.

Shredder grinned slyly. "On the contrary," he said. "*We're* going somewhere. And if you try to stop us, I'll cover him with this!" He held up a small glass container with an unmistakable green, glowing ooze inside.

Raph, Mike, and Leo faced off against Shredder. Don had one of his famous "ideas."

"Do you think I would be so foolish as to keep it all in one place?" Shredder gloated.

"Well, sort of," Leo said, stalling for time. He could see what Donnie was up to.

Don snuck around behind Shredder, behind the amplifier. He picked up one of the musicians' guitars. He turned the sound system up as high as it would go and strummed an E-major chord. It wasn't much musically, but it definitely was explosive. The amplifier behind Shredder blew up into a thousand pieces and the force of the explosion tossed the villain right through a plate-glass window.

Keno flew free of Shredder. The final battle could begin.

"Rock and roll!" Michaelangelo declared.

24

The Turtles rushed to the exit of the club to see what had become of Shredder. First, though, they saw what had become of Tokka and Rahzar. The wolf and snapping turtle, now just normal-sized, slept peacefully. They wouldn't cause anybody any more trouble.

The Turtles left the club and moved to the dock. The river water was dark and it was quiet—just the kind of situation designed to make a Turtle nervous.

"See anything?" Leo asked.

"Unh-unh," Don said.

"Well, dudes, I'd say that was pretty much a wrap!" Mike said.

The foursome slapped hands for their traditional high three.

"Cowabunga!" they agreed.

But they were wrong.

An enormous shadow crossed them. It was

Shredder times ten, rising up out of the muddy river water.

"That last vial of ooze!" Leonardo said.

The new, improved, mutated SuperShredder picked up a massive steel girder and hurled it at the Turtles. They got out of the way in time. The girder made a gigantic hole in the dock. The Turtles dashed down it, hoping to escape and save their lives. The bad news was that SuperShredder followed right after them.

"Any ideas?" Leonardo asked his brothers as they fled.

"How far is it to England?" Mike asked, looking out at the harbor.

But instead of heading out to the open water where SuperShredder would find and destroy them easily, they stayed in the understructure of the dock, bobbing in the dark and murky water. Leo reasoned that it would be harder for SuperShredder to capture them in the maze of beams. It was true, but it also gave SuperShredder more things to destroy as he proceeded.

There was a frightful creaking above. Don was the first to recognize that the real danger wasn't Shredder; it was the dock on top of them. "This dock isn't going to take much more. Leo maybe you can reason with him."

"Shredder!" Leonardo cried. "Listen to me! You'll kill us all!"

"Then, so be it!" SuperShredder declared. He continued his savage thrashing through the structure.

Suddenly a huge cement mixer broke through

the weakened dock above, and came crashing through the structure and straight into the water below. The Turtles knew the dock was about to go.

"We're pancakes!" Mike said.

"The true Ninja is a master of his environment, and himself. Don't forget. . . ." The collapse began. "We're turtles!!" Leonardo finished.

With those words the dock began to collapse completely. The structure groaned and cracked under its burden.

Leonardo took a header into the hole in the floor made by the cement mixer. His brothers followed.

The destruction of the dock was complete. It was like a row of dominoes tumbling or a house of cards falling. Concrete flooring folded and collapsed. Bricks spurted out like firecrackers. Hundreds of thousands of tons of debris fell on what had once been the dock.

Then there was silence.

Far out in the harbor, a turtle shell bobbed to the surface. Then another. A third, and finally the fourth. Then, one by one, the turtles lifted their heads from the water. They were safe!

Michaelangelo looked back at the totally destroyed building and dock. He thought what might have happened if he and his brothers hadn't been able to get out of there—fast.

"I've said it before and I'll say it again."

He didn't have to say it alone. His brothers said it with him. "God, I *love* being a turtle!"

"Look!" Don said. The four of them looked at the pile of wreckage where the dock had been. Was it possible that there was motion in the rubble. Could it be?

Suddenly, something did move. It was a giant hand, reaching out from under the mess.

"It can't be!" Mike said.

"Nobody could have survived that!"

Then, as they watched, the gigantic hand fell limply back into the heap.

"Not even Shredder," Leonardo said.

25 ═══════════

Splinter was alone in the subway den and he watched the TV intently. April was on the television screen.

". . . and in a bizarre final note to the mysterious disappearance of T.G.R.I., this message was delivered to the station earlier today." She picked up a piece of paper and began reading. " 'To Leonardo, Donatello, Michaelangelo, and Raphael: Thanks for your help, dudes.' Signed Professor Jordan Perry." She grinned slyly at the camera. "Of course, we can only guess at its meaning. And now this . . ."

Splinter clicked off the television with the remote. His four students were returning home. He could hear them chattering in the tunnel above.

The four Turtles were ready for some celebrating.

"Bo*dac*ious!" Leonardo said, dropping into the den.

"Os-ten-*tat*ious!" Raphael agreed, following Leo inside.

"Uhhh, *spac*ious!" Don added as he came down the ladder. His brothers looked at him curiously. He did sometimes seem to miss the point.

" 'Cowabunga' says it all, dudes," Mike told them, arriving last.

Splinter appeared pleased, but solemn. They gathered around him for his words of wisdom on the fierce battle they'd just fought—and won—against his greatest enemy.

"Were you seen?" Splinter asked.

The Turtles exchanged glances. What Splinter didn't know wouldn't hurt him.

"Of course not, Master Splinter," Leo assured him.

"We practice Ninja," Donatello reminded Splinter.

"The art of invisibility," Michaelangelo added.

Splinter picked up a newspaper from the table. He opened it up and showed it to them. On the front page was a very large picture of four Teenage Mutant Ninja Turtles on the stage at the Dockside Club. The headline read,

NINJA RAP IS BORN!

"Practice harder," Splinter said.

Without a word, the four Turtles began doing backflips.

"One . . . two . . . three . . ."